Every child sat on the floor of the hall with arms folded and legs crossed. No one had tidy hair and everyone had rosy red cheeks. The headmaster paced up and down on the platform. He told us how naughty it was to go out of the playground and into the park. He told us how very very naughty it was not to listen when a teacher blew a whistle. He told us how very very very naughty it was not to listen when he rang a bell. We all knew that anyway!

Even Naughtier Stories

Compiled by Barbara Ireson
Illustrated by Tony Ross

RED FOX

A Red Fox Book

Published by Random House Children's Books
20 Vauxhall Bridge Road, London SW1V 2SA
A division of Random House UK Ltd
London Melbourne Sydney Auckland
Johannesburg and agencies throughout the world

First published by Hutchinson's Children's Books 1990
Red Fox edition 1991
Reprinted 1992 (twice)

Text © in this collection Barbara Ireson 1990
Illustrations © Tony Ross 1990

Made and printed in Great Britain by
The Guernsey Press Co Ltd
Guernsey C.I.

ISBN 0 09 980890 0

Contents

Contents

Ultra-Violet Catastrophe!

Margaret Mahy

Sally's mother stood underneath a big tree looking up into its branches.

'Sally!' she called. 'Are you there, Sally?'

'She isn't here,' Sally called back. 'Something has eaten her. It's dangerous up here.'

'Sally, come down at once!' her mother called again.

Sally shut her eyes and answered, 'I'm not Sally. I'm Horrible Stumper the tree pirate.'

But it was no use. Horrible Stumper the tree pirate had to come down out of the leaves and the smell of spring and turn into Sally once more.

Sally was washed around the face and scrubbed around the knees. She had to take off her blue jeans and put on her best dress and her long white socks. Her hair was brushed until it shone and her ears went all red and hot. She was being taken to visit a cousin of her mother's called Aunt Anne Pringle.

Aunt Anne lived in the country, but not on a farm. Her house was called *Sunny Nook*, and it was full of things Sally was not allowed to touch.

'She doesn't like me even to *breathe*,' Sally said crossly. 'She fusses and fusses all the time and there's no one to play with.'

'You'll have to manage somehow,' replied her mother. 'Surely you can sit still for a couple of hours. I know Anne is fussy, and I know there are no children to play with, but you can't expect everything to suit you all the time. . . . Sometimes you have to suit other people. Oh dear, your knees still look dirty.'

'It's the scratches,' Sally explained. 'Knees are the worst part for getting scratched. I could paint faces on my knees and then the scratches wouldn't show.'

'Come on!' said Sally's mother in rather a sharp voice. 'Hurry up, or we'll be late.'

They caught the bus in time.

Sally had hoped that they would miss it.

Aunt Anne met them at the door of *Sunny Nook*. Sally could tell at once that she had not improved. She was tiny, and terribly clean and neat. She looked more like a freshly dusted china ornament than any real person. She smiled at Sally, and then talked over her head to her mother.

'I have Father staying with me for a month,' she said. 'It's rather awkward. Old men can be so difficult, and he's very set in his ways, you know. The things he says! Sometimes I don't understand just what he's getting at, he uses such funny, long words.'

Sally's mother made an I'm-sorry-to-hear-that clicking sound with her tongue.

They went into Aunt Anne's tiny sitting-room. There on the flowery couch was a very clean, scrubbed-and-scoured, washed-up and brushed-down, little old man.

Sally thought Aunt Anne must have rinsed him out, and then starched and ironed him, and *then* polished him with a soft cloth.

'This is Sally, Father,' said Aunt Anne. 'Do you remember hearing about Sally? I told you we had a dear little girl coming to visit us.'

Sally's mother thought she saw a Horrible Stumper-look coming on Sally's face again. She began to talk quickly. 'Sally, this is Great-Uncle Magnus Pringle.'

Great-Uncle Magnus looked at Sally from under his wrinkly eyelids. He said something very mysterious.

'Ultra-Violet Catastrophe to you, young lady.' His voice was loud for such a clean old man – loud but not crackly. It was rather like guns at sea.

'Oh, don't start talking rubbish!' said Aunt Anne fretfully. 'Look, why don't you two take each other for a walk down to the corner, while

3

we girls have a little chat by ourselves?'

Mother and Aunt Anne took Sally and Great-Uncle Magnus out of the house and pointed them down the road towards the corner.

'Be good and keep clean,' said Aunt Anne.

'Do look after each other,' called Sally's mother.

Sally and Great-Uncle Magnus walked along the country road in the country sunshine smelling the country smells of wet grass and cows.

They came to a thick dark hedge speckled with little white flowers.

Suddenly Great-Uncle Magnus stopped.

'Do you like to go through hedges?' he asked. '*I* do, and it's years since I've been through a good hedge.'

Sally stared at Great-Uncle Magnus, amazed at such thoughts in a great-uncle.

'I see a hole in this hedge,' went on Great-Uncle Magnus, 'and I'm going through it. . . . It would be a help to have you give me a hand up on the other side.'

'Shall I go first, then?' asked Sally. 'In case of danger?'

'That would be kind of you,' said Great-Uncle Magnus. 'I have this creaky knee, you see. It's a good knee, mind you. I've had it for years, but it *is* creaky.'

Sally scrambled through the hole in the hedge,

smelling its special hedge smell as she went. The hedge tried to hold on to her, as hedges do, but she got through safely. After her came Great-Uncle Magnus, breathing hard.

'Ah,' he said, as Sally helped him up, 'that was good. That was refreshing. Now what have we here?'

On the other side of the hedge the ground was swampy from yesterday's rain. In between the grass, muddy water was oozing. Grass tufts stuck out of puddles.

'It's a long time since I had a paddle,' said Great-Uncle Magnus thoughtfully.

'What are you doing?' cried Sally.

'Taking my shoes and socks off,' the great-uncle replied, and so he was.

Sally grinned. She sat down beside Great-Uncle Magnus and took off her shoes and her long, white socks, too. She had to help the great-uncle with a tightly tied shoe lace.

'She always ties my shoe laces as if she were choking my shoes to death,' said Great-Uncle Magnus.

Great-Uncle Magnus's pale feet sank greedily into the mud.

'Ah!' he sighed, 'there's something about mud, eh? Nothing else has quite that – that – *muddy* feel, has it?'

Sally was amazed again. She had not expected

to find a great-uncle who felt the same way about mud as she did.

'Ultra-Violet Catastrophe,' murmured the great-uncle to himself.

'What does that mean?' asked Sally boldly.

It's the *sound* I say it for, not the meaning,' Great-Uncle Magnus explained. 'Some people say, "Goodness gracious". That doesn't mean much – they say it for the sound. But *I* like to say something that sounds even better and more important.'

'Words usually mean some real thing,' said Sally carefully. 'For instance, I say "Horrible Stumper" and it means a tree pirate. Don't your good words mean anything?'

'They *do* mean something scientific,' admitted Great-Uncle Magnus. 'Something scientific and too hard to explain.' He started to paddle along through the grass and mud. He had a muddy patch on the back of his trousers where he had been sitting down.

'You see,' he said, as he went along, 'Annie's a good girl and she means well – but she treats me like one of her pot plants. She waters me and puts me in the sun and leaves me alone. Serve her right if I grew up the wall and put out flowers. After a while I begin to think I'm really turning into a pot plant, and then I sing to myself or use long words – "Ultra-Violet Catastrophe", I say, or, sometimes, "Seismological Singularity".'

'That's a *hard* one,' said Sally with great respect.

'Too hard for a pot plant!' Great-Uncle Magnus nodded. 'No mere pot plant would use words like that. *Then* I know I'm Magnus Pringle all the time.'

They came to a clear stream flowing over brown stones. On the bank above the stream a green tree spread wide, rough arms. Great-Uncle Magnus's sharp, old eyes looked up into the green arch above them.

'It's years since I climbed a tree, years and years,' said Great-Uncle Magnus. 'I'd climb this one if it wasn't for my fear of the tree pirates.'

'Oh, well – I'll just go up and check for you,' Sally offered eagerly. 'This is too good a tree to waste! And when I'm up, I can help you if your knee creaks or if it's too hard for you or anything.'

'There's nothing like a tree,' Great-Uncle Magnus remarked a few minutes later. 'It's good being up in a tree, up in the air and the leaves all around us. What do *you* think?'

'Ultra-Violet Catastrophe, *I* think,' answered Sally boldly.

'Just what I was thinking myself, Seismological Singularity!' said Great-Uncle Magnus. 'I think I'll sing a bit.'

He pointed his old nose to the sky and began to sing:

'Boiled beef and carrots,
Boiled beef and carrots.'

Sally felt very happy, sitting up there in the tree listening to Great-Uncle Magnus.

Everything felt very alive . . . the tree with its branches and bark and its spring leaves bright against the blue sky. Sally pointed her nose at the sky too, and felt the sun shine through the leaves in hot, spring freckles on her face. The tree at home and the tree here were like sunny rooms in open, rustling houses. She looked down at the stream below.

'Is it years and years since you made a dam across a creek?' asked Sally.

'How did you guess?' Great-Uncle Magnus said, wonderingly. 'It is certainly a long time ago. I see some good stones down there, too.'

Somehow Sally and Great-Uncle Magnus were not as tidy as they had been when they set out.

Making a dam did not improve things. When you are making a dam it is easy to get damp and muddy around the edges. They built a good dam out of mossy green and brown stones. The cunning water found a way over, or around, or through – keeping them busy and silent for quite a long time.

Then a sudden noise made Great-Uncle Magnus look up. He cleared his throat carefully.

'Sally,' he said, 'don't be frightened, but just look behind you and tell me what you see.'

Sally looked under her arm at the bank behind her. A large brown-and-white cow was standing there, watching them. She had a very young brown-and-white calf beside her. She had very sharp horns. As Sally looked, she put her head down and pointed her horns at them. She gave a grumbling, angry, 'Moo!'

'Having a new calf can make a cow very cross,' Great-Uncle Magnus said, gathering up his socks and shoes. 'Not that I'm frightened of a mere cow but still. . . .'

'A cow with a calf isn't as mere as other cows, I don't think,' said Sally, gathering up her socks and shoes, too.

The cow started to come down the bank at them. Sally and Great-Uncle Magnus moved quickly. Sally was amazed at the speed a great-uncle can put on when there is an angry cow coming down the bank after him.

There was no hedge on the other side of the creek, but there was a barbed-wire fence. Socks and shoes were tossed across. Then Sally scrambled over it. As she did so, she heard the hem of her dress tear open. A moment later Great-Uncle Magnus's trousers tore, too.

Sally and Great-Uncle Magnus stood staring at each other while the cow mooed angrily at them from the other side of the fence. Then her calf called, and she hurried back to it. And, at that very moment, like other anxious, mooing cows, Sally's mother and Aunt Anne were calling down the road.

Great-Uncle Magnus shook his head slowly. 'I can't see myself,' he said, 'but I don't think your mother is going to be pleased with *your* appearance.'

'I don't think Aunt Anne will be pleased with yours, either,' Sally told him. They were both wet and muddy and stained and torn.

There was a most terrible fuss!

'How *could* you, Father, how *could* you!' Aunt Anne cried.

'It just happened, Annie,' said Great-Uncle Magnus in a humble voice.

Aunt Anne made them stand on newspapers on the path, while she brushed them and cleaned them as well as she could.

'It's just as well you're going home at the end of the week,' she said to Great-Uncle Magnus. 'I couldn't stand another adventure like this!'

'Very sorry, Annie,' said Great-Uncle Magnus in his humble voice. He looked at Sally's mother. 'Why don't you and Sally come to see me when I go home?' he asked. 'I've got a little place by the beach, and a little boat I paddle around in. I catch a few fish from the end of the wharf. You wouldn't be bored.'

'We'd love to come,' said Sally's mother. (She wasn't as upset as Aunt Anne, being used to mud and torn skirts.) 'I can see you two get on well together,' she added.

'We've got a lot in common,' Great-Uncle Magnus agreed.

They had been so long on their walk there was scarcely time for Sally to have a bite to eat before getting ready to go home.

Sally and Great-Uncle Magnus looked at each other and could not find proper words to say goodbye in, even if it were only for a short time.

'Hurry, Sally, we'll miss the bus,' called her mother.

Sally suddenly knew the exact words to say. 'Ultra-Violet Catastrophe!' she called back, as her mother waved to Aunt Anne with one hand and tugged her with the other.

Great-Uncle Magnus brightened up. 'Horrible Stumper to *you*, young lady,' he replied. 'I wouldn't wish to go on a country walk with a better tree pirate than you yourself.'

My Naughty Little Sister and the Workmen

Dorothy Edwards

When my sister was a naughty little girl, she was very, very inquisitive. She was always looking and peeping into things that didn't belong to her. She used to open other people's cupboards and boxes just to find out what was inside.

Aren't you glad you're not inquisitive like that?

Well now, one day a lot of workmen came to dig up all the roads near our house, and my little sister was very interested in them. They were very nice men, but some of them had rather loud shouty voices sometimes. There were shovelling men, and picking men, and men with jumping-about things that went, 'ah-ah-ah-ah-ah-ah-aha-aaa', and men who drank tea out of jam pots, and men who cooked sausages over fires, and there was an old, old man who sat up all night when the other men had gone home, and who had lots of coats and scarves to keep him warm.

There were lots of things for my little

14

inquisitive sister to see, there were heaps of earth, and red lanterns for the old, old man to light at night time, and long poley things to keep the people from falling down the holes in the road, and workmen's huts, and many other things.

When the workmen were in our road, my little sister used to watch them every day. She used to lean over the gate and stare and stare, but when they went off to the next road she didn't see so much of them.

Well now, I will tell you about the inquisitive thing my little sister did one day, shall I?

Yes. Well, Bad Harry was my little sister's best boy-friend. Now this Bad Harry came one day to ask my mother if my little sister could go round to his house to play with him, and as Bad Harry's house wasn't far away, and as there were no roads to cross, my mother said my little sister could go.

So my little sister put on her hat and her coat, and her scarf and her gloves, because it was a nasty cold day, and went off with her best boy-friend to play with him.

They hurried along like good children until they came to the workmen in the next road, and then they went slow as slow, because there were so many things to see. They looked at this, and at that, and when they got past the workmen they found a very curious thing.

By the road there was a tall hedge, and under the tall hedge there was a mackintoshy bundle.

Now this mackintoshy bundle hadn't anything to do with Bad Harry, and it hadn't anything to do with my naughty little sister, yet, do you know, they were so inquisitive they stopped and looked at it.

They had such a good look at it that they had to get right under the hedge to see, and when they got very near it they found it was an old mackintosh wrapped round something or other inside.

Weren't they naughty? They should have gone straight home to Bad Harry's mother's house, shouldn't they? But they didn't. They stayed and looked at the mackintoshy bundle.

And they opened it. They really did. It wasn't their bundle, but they opened it wide under the hedge, and do you know what was inside it? I know you aren't an inquisitive meddlesome child, but would you like to know?

Well, inside the bundle there were lots and lots of parcels and packages tied up in red handkerchiefs, and brown paper, and newspaper, and instead of putting them back again like nice children those little horrors started to open all those parcels, and inside those parcels there were lots of things to eat!

There were sandwiches, and cakes, and meat

and cold cooked fish, and eggs and goodness knows what-all.

Weren't those bad children surprised? They couldn't think how all those sandwiches and things could have got into that old mackintosh.

Then Bad Harry said, 'Shall we eat them?' You remember he was a greedy lad. But my little sister said, 'No, it's picked-up food.' My little sister knew that my mother had told her never, never to eat picked-up food. You see she was good about *that*.

Only she was very bad after that, because she said, 'I know, let's play with it.'

So they took all those sandwiches and cakes and meat-pies and cold cooked fish and eggs and they laid them out across the path and made them into pretty patterns on the ground. Then Bad Harry threw a sandwich at my little sister and she threw a meat-pie at him, and they began to have a lovely game.

And then do you know what happened? A big roary voice called out, 'What do you think you're doing with our dinners, you monkeys – you?' And there was a big workman coming towards them, looking so cross and angry that those two bad children screamed and screamed, and because the workman was so roary they turned and ran and ran down the road and the workman ran after them as cross as cross. Weren't they frightened?

When they got back to where the other workmen were digging, those children were more frightened than ever, because the big workman shouted to all the other workmen about what these naughty children had done with their dinners.

Yes, those poor workmen had put all their dinners under the hedge in the old mackintosh to keep them dry and safe until dinner-time. As well as being frightened, Bad Harry and my naughty little sister were very ashamed.

They were so ashamed that they did a most silly thing. When they heard the big workman telling the others about their dinners, those silly children ran and hid themselves in one of the pipes that the workmen were putting in the road.

My naughty little sister went first, and old Bad Harry went in after her. Because my naughty little sister was so frightened she wriggled in and in the pipe, and Bad Harry came wriggling in after her, because he was frightened too.

And then a dreadful thing happened to my naughty little sister. That Bad Harry *stuck in the pipe* and he couldn't get any further. He was quite a round fat boy, you see, and he stuck fast as fast in the pipe.

Then didn't those sillies howl and howl.

My little sister howled because she didn't want to go on and on down the roadmen's pipe on her own, and Bad Harry howled becuase he couldn't move at all.

It was all terrible of course, but the roary workman rescued them very quickly. He couldn't reach Bad Harry with his arm, but he got a good long hooky iron thing, and he hooked it in Bad Harry's belt, and he pulled and pulled, and presently he pulled Bad Harry out of the pipe. Wasn't it a good thing they had a hooky iron? And wasn't it a *very* good thing that bad Harry had a strong belt on his coat?

When Bad Harry was out, my little sister wriggled back and back, and came out too, and when she saw all the poor workmen who wouldn't have any dinner, she cried and cried, and told them what a sorry girl she was.

She told the workmen that she and Bad Harry hadn't known the mackintoshy bundle was their dinners, and Bad Harry said he was sorry too and they were really so truly ashamed that the big workman said, 'Well, never mind this time. It's pay-day today, so we can send the boy for fish and chips instead,' and he told my little sister not to cry any more.

So my little sister stopped crying, and she and Bad Harry said they would never, never meddle and be inquisitive again.

Jane's Mansion

Robin Klein

Jane liked pretending to be grander than she really was. One day she was walking home from school with a new girl named Kylie, and showing off as usual.

'We have five Siamese cats at our house. And a special iced lemonade tap.'

Kylie dawdled, hoping to be invited in.

'I'd ask you in,' said Jane, 'but my mother's overseas. She's a famous opera singer.'

'Wow!' said Kylie.

'She's singing in Paris. Our housekeeper, Mrs Grid, is looking after me. Our house has twenty-five rooms full of Persian carpets and antique furniture.'

Kylie looked at Jane's house, thinking that a house containing such splendours would somehow look different.

'Don't take any notice of the front view,' said Jane. 'My Dad built it like that to trick burglars.

22

Inside it's different. My father is a millionaire.'

She waved goodbye airily and went inside.

The house certainly was different inside!

The living room was carpeted with gorgeous rugs, and had a silver fountain labelled 'iced lemonade'. The cane furniture had been replaced by carved oak.

'*Mum*! Did we win the pools?' Jane yelled

excitedly! Her mother wasn't home, but a note had been left in the kitchen. It read:

FROM PARIS GOING TO MILAN TO SING TOSCA, AFTER THAT VIENNA. HOUSEKEEPER WILL LOOK AFTER YOU, LOVE, MUM.

Jane read the note and then phoned the factory where her Dad worked. A voice said, 'Sorry it's not possible to speak to Mr Lawson. He's overseas inspecting all his oil wells, diamond mines and banks.'

It was Jane's turn to say Wow!

She went into her room to change. Normally her room was a clutter of dropped clothes, unmade bed, and overdue library books. But now it was magnificent. It had a four poster-bed, and a TV set in the ceiling. Jane was so impressed that she hung up her school dress instead of letting it lie like a gingham puddle on the floor.

She ran all around the splendid house looking at everything. It was amazing that such a vast mansion could fit into an ordinary surburban block. The back yard was too stupendous to be called that. There was a sunken pool in a huge lawn. She couldn't even find the fences that separated her house from the neighbours'. 'Not that I'd want to, now I'm a millionaire's daughter,' she thought smugly.

At six a brass gong summoned her for dinner at a long table lit by a candelabrum. There was one place set. 'Don't put your elbows on the table, Miss Jane,' somebody strict said. It was Mrs Grid, the housekeeper, and she was just as impressive as the house.

Jane couldn't even resist showing off to her. 'I've got to go to the Youth Club,' she said when she had finished dinner. 'I won every single trophy. It's Presentation Night.'

'I'll have Norton bring the car round to the front door,' Mrs Grid said.

Jane waited by the front steps. A huge car drove up, and a uniformed man held the door open for her. Jane remembered telling Kylie that she had a chauffeur. She felt very important being driven to Youth Club like that. Everyone's parents had come for Presentation Night. She regretted that hers were overseas, specially when the club president announced, 'Trophy for the most advanced member – Jane Lawson.'

No sooner had Jane received the trophy and sat down than the president said, 'Cup awarded for callisthenics – Jane Lawson', and she had to go back. She won every single prize, but it wasn't nearly as nice as she thought it would be. After her tenth trip to the stage, the clapping sounded forced, and most of the parents were glaring at her.

When she got home she showed the trophies to Mrs Grid.

Mrs Grid only said, 'All that silver will take a lot of polishing. I've already got enough to do looking after this mansion.'

Next morning her father cabled that he was in Brazil buying coffee plantations. Jane rang Kylie to brag.

'My Dad bought me a pair of skates,' Kylie said excitedly. 'Want to come round and see?'

'Skates are nothing,' Jane scoffed. '*My* father bought *me* a *horse*.'

There was a loud neighing at the window, and she put the phone back and went to look. A large horse was trotting round in the garden. 'Put your horse back in the stable at once,' said Mrs Grid crossly.

'I don't want to,' said Jane, but Mrs Grid looked at her so sternly that she lied quickly, 'We have a groom to look after my horse.'

A bandy-legged man in jodphurs appeared and led the horse away. Jane was relieved, because she was really scared of horses.

She went for another walk around her mansion, finding a whole lot of things she'd lied into existence in past conversations with people. There was a trained circus poodle, a crystal bathtub with goldfish swimming round the sides, a real little theatre complete with spotlights, a gymnasium in the basement, and five Siamese cats. She had a marvellous time playing with all that, but she was starting to feel lonely. Mrs Grid was too busy and crotchety to be company. Jane rang Kylie again.

'Come round and I'll let you ride my horse,' she offered.

'You wouldn't come round to see my skates,' Kylie pointed out, offended.

'We've got a real theatre and a crystal bath with goldfish swimming round the sides. Come round to my house and play,' Jane begged.

'I'd better not,' said Kylie.

'Why not?'

'Your house sounds too grand. I'd be scared of breaking something valuable. I'd better just play with you at school.' She hung up.

Jane sat and looked at all her trophies, and tried to feel proud. But she knew very well she hadn't really won any of those glittering things. She'd only got them by lying.

She missed her parents dreadfully, and remembered that this weekend her Dad had intended to make her a tree house. But he was in Brazil instead. 'Where's my shell collection and my pig I made out of a lemon?' she asked Mrs Grid, starting to cry.

'I threw all that rubbish out,' said Mrs Grid. 'And there's no point moping. Your parents have to work very hard to keep you in the manner you prefer. You'll just have to wait till Christmas to see them. I daresay they'll be able to drop in for a few minutes then.'

'I'm getting my own speedboat for Christmas,' Jane boasted, lying automatically through her tears.

'That reminds me,' said Mrs Grid. 'This telegram arrived for you.'

STATE MODEL AND COLOUR PREFERENCE FOR SPEEDBOAT WILL HAVE DELIVERED DEC. 25 LOVE ABSENT PARENTS.

Jane bawled louder.

'Just as well you're going away to boarding school tomorrow,' Mrs Grid said. 'So I won't have to put up with that awful noise.'

Jane was shocked into silence. She remembered lying to the neighbours that she'd won a scholarship to boarding school. She didn't want to go. She wanted her own house to be the way it usually was, with her own nice comfortable parents in it.

'You could pack your things for boarding school now,' said Mrs Grid. 'I'll get Norton to drive you there early.'

Jane jumped up. She ran out of the house and down the street to Kylie's. When Kylie opened the door, Jane babbled feverishly, 'We don't have a swimming pool, lemonade tap, horse, groom, miniature theatre or five Siamese cats, and I'm not going to boarding school. My Dad's not a millionaire, he's a fitter and turner. And my mum can't sing for toffee. We haven't got any antiques or Persian carpets, and I didn't win any trophies at Youth Club. I'll never tell any more lies ever again! And we haven't got a housekeeper, or a chauffeur called Norton. Please come up to my house to play, Kylie.'

'All right,' said Kylie. 'I knew you were lying, anyhow.'

They went back to Jane's house, and Jane drew a big breath and opened the door. It opened into her usual living room with its old cane furniture, and she could hear her Mum in the kitchen, singing off-key. Jane ran and hugged her. 'Where's Dad?' she asked anxiously.

'Just gone up to get the timber for your tree house,' said her mother. 'You can take some scones into your room if you like.'

'My room hasn't got a four-poster bed or a TV set in the ceiling,' Jane said to Kylie before she opened the door.

'I didn't think it had,' said Kylie.

They ate their scones while they looked at Jane's shell collection and the pig she had made out of a lemon. The scones tasted much nicer than

Mrs Grid's cooking. 'We haven't got a gymnasium in the basement or a poodle or a speedboat either,' said Jane. 'I tell a lot of lies.'

Her mother came to collect her scone plate. She was cross about something.

'Who stripped the enamel off the bath tub and put goldfish in the sides?' she demanded.

Having Fun

René Goscinny

This afternooon I ran into Alec on my way to school and he said, 'Suppose we play truant?' I told him that would be naughty and our teacher wouldn't be pleased, and Dad had told me you had to work if you wanted to get on in life and be an airman, and Mum would be sad and it was wicked to tell lies. Alec reminded me it was arithmetic this afternoon, so I said, 'OK', and we didn't go to school.

We ran off in the opposite direction instead. Alec started puffing and blowing and he couldn't keep up. I ought to mention that Alec is my fat friend who's always eating, so of course he isn't too good at running, and I happen to be really great at the forty metres sprint, which is the length of the school playground. 'Hurry up, Alec!' I said. 'I can't!' said Alec. And he did a lot more puffing and then stopped entirely. I told him it was no good staying here, or our Mums and Dads might see us and not let us have any pudding, and then there were the school inspectors who'd put us in prison and keep us on bread and water. When Alec heard this it made him much braver and he started running so fast that I could hardly keep up myself.

We stopped a long way off, just past the nice grocer's where Mum buys the strawberry jam I like. 'We'll be safe here,' said Alec, and he took some biscuits out of his pocket and started eating them, because, he told me, running after lunch like that had made him hungry.

'This is a good idea of yours, Alec!' I said. 'When I think of the others doing arithmetic at school I could laugh my head off!' 'Me too,' said Alec, so we laughed. When we'd finished laughing I asked Alec what we were going to do now. 'No idea,' said Alec. 'We could go to the pictures.' That was a great idea too, only we didn't have any money. When we turned out our pockets we found string, marbles, two elastic bands and some crumbs. The crumbs were in Alec's pocket and he ate them. 'Oh well,' I said, 'never mind, even if we can't go to the pictures the others would rather be here with us!' 'You bet!' said Alec. 'Anyway, I wasn't really all that keen to see *The Sheriff's Revenge*.' 'Nor me,' I said. 'I mean, it's only a Western.' And we walked past the cinema to look at the stills outside. There was a cartoon film on too.

'Suppose we went to the square gardens?' I said. 'We could make a ball out of old paper and have a game.' Alec said that wasn't a bad idea, only there was a man in charge of the square gardens and if he saw us he'd ask us why we weren't at school and he'd take us away and lock us in a dungeon and keep us on bread and water. Just thinking of it made Alec feel hungry, and he got a cheese sandwich out of his satchel. We went on walking down the road, and when Alec had finished his sandwich he said, 'Well, the others at school aren't having fun, are they?' 'No fear,' I said, 'and anyway it's too late to go now, we'd get punished.'

We looked in the shop windows. Alec told me what all the things in the pork butcher's window were, and then we went to make faces in the mirrors which are in the windows of the shop selling perfume and stuff, but we went away again because we saw the people inside the shop looking at us and they seemed rather surprised. We looked at the clocks in the jeweller's window and it was still awfully early. 'Great!' I said. 'Plenty of time to have fun before we go home.' We were tired with all this walking, so Alec suggested going to the bit of waste ground, there's no one around there and you can sit down. The waste ground is really good. We had fun throwing stones at the empty tin cans. Then we got tired of throwing stones so we sat down and Alec started on a ham sandwich out of his satchel. It was his last sandwich. 'They must be in the middle of doing sums at school,' said Alec. 'No, they aren't,' I said. 'It'll be break by now.' 'Huh! You don't think break is any fun, do you?' Alec asked me. 'You bet I don't!' I said, and then I started to cry. Let's face it, it wasn't all that much fun here all on our own, with nothing to do, and having to hide, and I was right to want to go to school even if it *was* arithmetic and if I hadn't gone and met Alec I'd be having break now and I'd be playing marbles and cops and robbers and I'm very good at marbles. 'Why are you howling like that?' asked Alec. I said, 'It's all your fault I can't play cops and robbers.' Alec lost his temper. 'I didn't *ask* you to come with me,' he said, 'and what's more if you'd said you wouldn't come I'd have gone to school too so it's all your fault.' 'Oh really?' I said to Alec in a sarcastic voice Dad uses to Mr Billings who lives next door and likes to annoy Dad. 'Yes, really,' said Alec, just the same way Mr Billings says it to Dad, and we had a fight, just like Dad and Mr Billings.

When we'd finished our fight it started raining, so we went away from the waste ground because there wasn't anywhere to shelter from the rain, and my Mum doesn't like me to stay out in the wet and I almost never disobey my Mum.

Alec and I went to stand by the jeweller's shop window with the clocks in it. It was raining hard and we were all alone there and it wasn't that much fun. We waited till it was time to go home.

When I got home Mum said I looked so pale and tired that I could stay away from school tomorrow if I liked, and I said no and Mum was very surprised.

The thing is, when Alec and I tell the others at school tomorrow what fun we had they'll be green with envy!

Pierre

*a cautionary tale in Five Chapters
and a Prologue*

Maurice Sendak

Prologue
There was once a boy
named Pierre
who would only say,
'I don't care!'
Read his story,
my friend,
for you'll find
at the end
that a suitable
moral lies there.

Chapter I
One day
his mother said
when Pierre
climbed out of bed,
'Good morning,
darling boy,
you are
my only joy.'
Pierre said,
'I don't care!'
'What would you
like to eat?'
'I don't care!'
'Some lovely
cream of wheat?'

'I don't care!'
'Don't sit backwards
on your chair!'

'I don't care!'
'Or pour syrup
on your hair.'

'I don't care!'
'You are acting
like a clown.'
'I don't care!'
'And we have
to go to town.'

'I don't care!'
'Don't you want
to come, my dear?'
'I don't care!'
'Would you rather
stay right here?'
'I don't care!'
So his mother
left him there.

Chapter 2
His father said,
'Get off your head
or I'll march you
up to bed!'
Pierre said,
'I don't care!'
'I would think
that you could see –'
'I don't care!'
'Your head is where
your feet should be!'
'I don't care!'

'If you keep standing
upside down –'
'I don't care!'
'we'll never ever
get to town.'
'I don't care!'
'If only you would
say I CARE.'
'I don't care!'
'I'd let you fold
the folding chair.'

So his parents left him
there.
They didn't take him
anywhere.

Chapter 3
Now, as the night
began to fall
a hungry lion
paid a call.
He looked Pierre
right in the eye

and asked him
if he'd like to die.

Pierre said,
'I don't care!'
'I can eat you,
don't you see?'
'I don't care!'
'And you will be
inside of me.'
'I don't care!'
'Then you'll never
have to bother –'
'I don't care!'
'With a mother
and a father.'
'I don't care!'
'Is that all
you have to say?'
'I don't care!'
'Then I'll eat you,
if I may.'
'I don't care!'

So the lion
ate Pierre.

Chapter 4
Arriving home
at six o'clock,
his parents had
a dreadful shock!
They found the lion
sick in bed
and cried,
'Pierre is surely dead!'
They pulled the lion
by the hair,
They hit him
with the folding chair.
His mother asked,
'Where is Pierre?'
The lion answered,
'I don't care!'
His father said,
'Pierre's in there!'

Chapter 5
They rushed the lion
into town.
The doctor shook him
up and down.
And when the lion

gave a roar –
Pierre fell out
upon the floor.
He rubbed his eyes
and scratched his head
and laughed
because he wasn't dead.
His mother cried
and held him tight.
His father asked,
'Are you alright?'
Pierre said,
'I am feeling fine,
please take me home,
it's half past nine.'
The lion said,

'If you would care
to climb on me,
I'll take you there.'
Then everyone
looked at Pierre
who shouted,
'Yes, indeed I care!!'

The lion took them
home to rest
and stayed on
as a week-end guest.

The moral of Pierre
is: CARE!

Mr Miacca

Amabel Williams

Tommy Grimes was sometimes a good boy, and sometimes a bad boy, and when he was a bad boy, he was a very bad boy.

His mother used to say to him:

'Tommy, Tommy, be a good boy, and don't go out of our street, or else Mr Miacca will get you.'

But still, on the days when he was a bad boy he would go out of the street. One day, sure enough, he had scarcely got round the corner, when Mr Miacca caught him and popped him into a bag, upside down, and took him off to his house.

When Mr Miacca got Tommy inside the house, he pulled him out of the bag and set him down, and felt his arms and legs.

'You're rather tough,' says he, 'but you're all I've got for supper, and you'll not taste bad boiled. But, body o'me, I've forgotten the herbs, and it's bitter you'll taste without herbs. Sally! Here, I say, Sally!' And he called Mrs Miacca.

So Mrs Miacca came out of another room and said, 'What d'ye want, my dear?'

'Oh, here's a fine little boy for supper,' said Mr Miacca, 'but I've forgotten the herbs. Mind him, will ye, while I go for them.'

'All right, my love,' says Mrs Miacca, and off he goes.

Then Tommy Grimes said to Mrs Miacca, 'Does Mr Miacca always have little boys for supper?'

'Mostly, my dear,' said Mrs Miacca, 'if little boys are bad enough, and come his way.'

'And don't you have anything else but boy-meat?' No pudding?' asked Tommy.

'Ah, I loves pudding,' says Mrs Miacca, 'but it's not often the likes of us gets pudding.'

'Why, my mother is making a pudding this very day,' said Tommy Grimes, 'and I'm sure she'll give you some, if I asked her. Shall I run and get some?'

'Now, that's a thoughtful boy,' said Mrs Miacca, 'only don't be long and be sure to be back in time for supper.'

So off Tommy pelted, and right glad he was to get off! For many a long day he was as good as good could be, and never went round the corner out of the street.

But somehow, he couldn't always remember to be good. And one day he went round the corner

again and, as luck would have it, he hadn't scarcely got round it when Mr Miacca grabbed him up, popped him in his bag, and took him home.

When he got there, Mr Miacca dropped him out, and when he saw who it was he said, 'Ah, you're the youngster that served me and my missus such a shabby trick, leaving us without any supper! Well, you shan't do it again. I'll watch over you myself. Here, get under the sofa, and I'll sit on it and watch the pot boil for you.'

So poor Tommy Grimes had to creep under the sofa, and Mr Miacca sat on it and waited for the pot to boil. And they waited, and they waited, but still the pot didn't boil, till at last Mr Miacca got tired of waiting, and he said, 'Here, you under there, I'm not going to wait any longer. Put out your leg, and I'll stop you giving me the slip.'

So Tommy put out a leg, and Mr Miacca got out his chopper, and chopped it off, and popped it in the pot. Suddenly he calls out:

'Sally, my dear! Sally!' and nobody answered. So he went into the next room to look for Mrs Miacca, and while he was there, Tommy crept out from under the sofa and ran out of the door. For you see, it wasn't his own leg, but the leg of the sofa that he had put out.

So Tommy Grimes ran home and never went round the corner again until he was old enough to go alone.

The Naughtiest Story of All

Dorothy Edwards

This is such a very terrible story about my
naughty little sister that I hardly know how to tell
it to you. It is all about one Christmas-time when
I was a little girl, and my naughty little sister was
a very little girl.

Now, my naughty little sister was very pleased
when Christmas began to draw near, because she
liked all the excitement of the plum-puddings and
the turkeys, and the crackers and the holly, and
all the Christmassy-looking shops, but there was
one very awful thing about her – she didn't like to
think about Father Christmas at all – she said he
was a *horrid old man*!

There – I knew you would be shocked at that.
But she did. And she said she wouldn't put up her
stockings for him.

My mother told my naughty little sister what a
good old man Father Christmas was, and how he
brought the toys along on Christmas Eve, but my

naughty little sister said, 'I don't care. And I don't want that nasty old man coming to our house.'

Well now, that was bad enough, wasn't it? But the really dreadful thing happened later on.

This is the dreadful thing; one day, my school-teacher said that a Father Christmas Man would be coming to the school to bring presents for all the children, and my teacher said that the Father Christmas Man would have toys for all our little brothers and sisters as well, if they cared to come along for them. She said that there would be a real Christmas tree with candles on it, and sweeties and cups of tea and biscuits for our mothers.

Wasn't that a nice thought? Well now, when I told my little sister about the Christmas tree, she said 'Oh, nice!'

And when I told her about the sweeties she said, 'Very, very nice!' But when I told her about the Father Christmas Man, she said, 'Don't want *him*, nasty old man.'

Still, my mother said, 'You can't go to the Christmas tree without seeing him, so if you don't want to see him all that much, you will have to stay at home.'

But my naughty little sister did want to go, very much, so she said, 'I will go, and when the horrid Father Christmas Man comes in, I will close my eyes.'

47

So, we all went to the Christmas tree together, my mother and I, and my naughty little sister.

When we got to the school, my naughty little sister was very pleased to see all the pretty paper-chains that we had made in school hung all round the classrooms, and when she saw all the little lanterns, and the holly and all the robin-redbreast drawings pinned on the blackboards she smiled and smiled. She was very smily at first.

All the mothers, and the little brothers and sisters who were too young for school sat down in chairs and desks, and all the big schoolchildren acted a play for them.

My little sister was very excited to see all the children dressed up as fairies and robins and elves and Bo-peeps and things, and she clapped her hands very hard, like the grown-ups did, to show that she was enjoying herself. And she still smiled.

Then, when some of the teachers came round with bags of sweets, tied up in pretty coloured paper, my little sister smiled even more, and she sang too when all the children sang. She sang, 'Away in a manger,' because she knew the words very well. When she didn't know the words of some of the singing, she 'la-la'd'.

After all the singing, the teachers put out the lights, and took away the big screen from a corner of the room, and there was the Christmas tree, all lit up with candles and shining with silvery stuff, and little shiny coloured balls. There were lots of toys on the tree, and all the children cheered and clapped.

Then the teachers put the lights on again, and blew out the candles, so that we could all go and look at the tree. My little sister went too. She looked at the tree, and she looked at the toys, and she saw a specially nice doll with a blue dress on, and she said, 'For me.'

My mother said, 'You must wait and see what you are given.'

Then the teachers called out, 'Back to your seats, everyone, we have a visitor coming.' So all the children went back to their seats, and sat still and waited and listened.

And, as we waited and listened, we heard a tinkle-tinkle bell noise, and then the schoolroom door opened, and in walked the Father Christmas Man. My naughty little sister had forgotten all about him, so she hadn't time to close her eyes before he walked in. However, when she saw him, my little sister stopped smiling and began to be stubborn.

The Father Christmas Man was very nice. He said he hoped we were having a good time, and we all said, 'Yes,' except my naughty little sister – she didn't say a thing.

Then he said, 'Now, one at a time, children; and I will give each one of you a toy.'

So, first of all each schoolchild went up for a toy, and my naughty little sister still didn't shut her eyes because she wanted to see who was going to have the specially nice doll in the blue dress. But none of the schoolchildren had it.

Then Father Christmas began to call the little brothers and sisters up for presents, and, as he didn't know their names, he just said, 'Come along, sonny,' if it were a boy, and 'come along, girlie,' if it were a girl. The Father Christmas Man let the little brothers and sisters choose their own toys off the tree.

When my naughty little sister saw this, she was so worried about the specially nice doll, that she thought she would just go up and get it. She said, 'I don't like the horrid old beardy man, but I do like that nice doll.'

So, my naughty little sister got up without being asked to, and she went right out to the front where the Father Christmas Man was standing, and she said, 'That doll, please,' and pointed to the doll she wanted.

The Father Christmas Man laughed and all the teachers laughed, and the other mothers and the schoolchildren, and all the little brothers and sisters. My mother did not laugh because she was so shocked to see my naughty little sister going out without being asked to.

The Father Christmas Man took the specially

nice doll off the tree, and handed it to my naughty little sister and he said, 'Well now, I hear you don't like me very much, but won't you just shake hands?' and my naughty little sister said, 'No.' But she took the doll all the same.

The Father Christmas Man put out his nice old hand for her to shake and be friends, and do you know what that naughty bad girl did? *She bit his hand*. She really and truly did. Can you think of anything more dreadful and terrible? She bit Father Christmas's good old hand, and then she turned and ran and ran out of the school with all the children staring after her, and her doll held very tight in her arms.

The Father Christmas Man was very nice, he said it wasn't a hard bite, only a frightened one, and he made all the children sing songs together.

When my naughty little sister was brought back by my mother, she said she was very sorry, and the Father Christmas Man said, 'That's all right, old lady,' and because he was so smily and nice to her, my funny little sister went right up to him and gave him a big 'sorry' kiss, which pleased him very much.

And she hung her stocking up after all, and that kind man remembered to fill it for her.

My little sister kept the specially nice doll until she was quite grown-up. She called it Rosy-Primrose, and although she was sometimes bad-tempered with it, she really loved it very much indeed.

Did I Ever Tell You About the Time When the School Fence was Broken Down?

Iris Grender

One night there was a terrible gale. When we went to school in the morning we looked at a place where the school fence had broken down. Then the whistle went and it was time to go into school.

At playtime the hole in the fence was still there. Two boys went through the hole and ran across the park behind the playground.

We all went through the hole in the fence. Soon the playground was quite empty. A teacher came out and blew her whistle. Everyone pretended they couldn't hear the whistle. They just ran and ran and ran across the great wide park.

It was lovely running about in the park. The teacher began chasing the children and blowing her whistle at the same time. She didn't catch anyone, because the park was so enormous.

Another teacher came out and joined in the chase. She caught three girls and sent them back

into the playground. Then the headmaster came out and rang a bell. We still pretended we couldn't hear.

By the time we had all been rounded up, the morning was nearly over. There was just ten minutes of morning school left before lunch. Every child sat on the floor of the hall with arms folded and legs crossed. No one had tidy hair and everyone had rosy red cheeks, The headmaster paced up and down on the platform. He told us how naughty it was to go out of the playground and into the park. He told us how very very naughty it was not to listen when a teacher blew a whistle. He told us how very very very naughty it was not to listen when he rang a bell. We all knew that anyway!

The school caretaker mended the broken-down fence and after that we only played in the playground. Running about in the park is much more exciting than running about in the playground. It's even more exciting when a teacher is chasing you and trying to catch everyone at once!

The Christmas List

Margaret Rettich

Wolfgang and Susanne had written a number of things on their Christmas list, but one wish they underlined with thick, red-pencil lines: 'One night we'd like to stay up for as long as we want to.'

'Why not?' Mama and Papa said.

They celebrated Christmas Eve together, there were lots of presents, they had something good to eat, and when it was time, Papa and Mama said, 'We're tired now and we're going to bed. Good night.'

'That's right,' said Susanne, 'and don't forget to brush your teeth.'

'And don't read any more!' cried Wolfgang after them.

'We're much too tired for that,' said Mama and yawned.

When Wolfgang and Susanne were alone, they jumped into chairs and stretched out their legs. Then they ate lots of marzipan. Susanne decided she should cover her parents up and give them a good night kiss. She did so, and Mama and Papa let themselves enjoy it.

Then Wolfgang and Susanne went back to the living room and turned on the television. A choir sang endless Christmas carols, which was boring. On another channel there was news and the weather report.

'Why isn't there any children's programme?' asked Susanne.

'Just think,' said Wolfgang, 'all the children are in bed now.'

That pleased them very much.

They turned the television off again and went into the kitchen. In the refrigerator there were lots of good things, but they weren't hungry. They only drank some soda and went back to the living room. They sat down again.

'Terrific when you can stay up late,' said Wolfgang. Susanne nodded and yawned.

They read the books that they had been given as presents and then ate some more marzipan. Susanne got more soda from the kitchen, and since she had forgotton the glasses, they drank out of the bottle. Wolfgang spilled the soda on his sweater; it was cold and sticky. He pulled it off and tried Papa's new pyjamas on. Susanne thought he looked funny. Mama had received a slip, which she tried on.

'Hah, we're ghosts,' she whispered. She stuck her head through the door to her parents' bedroom, but Mama and Papa were sound asleep, so Wolfgang and Susanne withdrew.

They tried the television again. On every channel there was whistling and sparkling.

'It's broken,' said Susanne.

'Don't be silly. They've stopped for the night. All the grown-ups are in bed now. Who would they broadcast for?'

'For us, for instance!' answered Susanne. She sat very straight in her chair.

Wolfgang turned the set off again. It was very quiet.

Once the cupboard creaked.

The light was very bright.

'How long do you want to stay up, anyhow?' asked Susanne.

'Till morning,' said Wolfgang.

Their eyes burned so terribly that he turned the lamp off. He tripped over the soda bottle and fell against Susanne's chair. She pulled his hair, and it hurt. So he pinched her arm.

Susanne ran away from Wolfgang and hid in her bed. Wolfgang crept quickly under his covers so that Susanne couldn't find him.

When they woke up, it was dark outside again. Papa and Mama had been up for a long time. They had had breakfast, had gone for a walk, had

had visitors, watched some television, and just done nothing.

Christmas Day was over.

The Family Dog

Judy Blume

Nobody ever came right out and said that Fudge was the reason that my father lost the Juicy-O account. But I thought about it. My father said he was glad to be rid of Mr Yarby. Now he could spend more time on his other clients – like the Toddle-Bike company. My father was in charge of their new TV commercial.

I thought maybe he could use me in it since I know how to stand on my head. But he said he wasn't planning on having any head-standers in the commercial.

I learned to stand on my head in gym class. I'm pretty good at it too. I can stay up for as long as three minutes. I showed my mother, my father and Fudge how I can do it right in the living room. They were all impressed. Especially Fudge. He wanted to do it too. So I turned him upside down and tried to teach him. But he always tumbled over backwards.

Right after I learned to stand on my head Fudge stopped eating. He did it suddenly. One day he was fine and the next day nothing. 'No eat,' he told my mother.

She didn't pay too much attention to him until the third day. When he still refused to eat she got upset. 'You've got to eat, Fudgie,' she said. 'You want to grow up to be big and strong, don't you?'

'No grow!' Fudge said.

That night my mother told my father how worried she was about Fudge. So my father did tricks for him while my mother stood over his chair trying to get some food into his mouth. But nothing worked. Not even juggling oranges.

Finally my mother got the brilliant idea of me standing on my head while she fed Fudge. I wasn't very excited about standing on my head in the kitchen. The floor is awfully hard in there. But my mother begged me. She said, 'It's very important for Fudge to eat. Please help us, Peter.'

So I stood on my head. When Fudge saw me upside down he clapped his hands and laughed. When he laughs he opens his mouth. That's when my mother stuffed some baked potato into it.

But the next morning I put my foot down. 'No! I don't want to stand on my head in the kitchen. Or anywhere else!' I added. 'And if I don't hurry I'll be late for school.'

'Don't you care if your brother starves?'

'No!' I told her.

'Peter! What an awful thing to say.'

'Oh . . . he'll eat when he gets hungry. Why don't you just leave him alone!'

That afternoon when I came home from school I found my brother on the kitchen floor playing with boxes of cereals and raisins and dried apricots. My mother was begging him to eat.

'No, no, no!' Fudge shouted. He made a

terrible mess, dumping everything on the floor.

'Please stand on your head, Peter,' my mother said. 'It's the only way he'll eat.'

'No!' I told her. 'I'm not going to stand on my head any more.' I went into my room and slammed the door. I played with Dribble until suppertime. Nobody ever worries about me the way they worry about Fudge. If I decided not to eat they'd probably never even notice!

That night during dinner Fudge hid under the kitchen table. He said, 'I'm a doggie. Woof . . . woof . . . woof!'

It was hard to eat with him under the table pulling on my legs. I waited for my father to say something. But he didn't.

Finally my mother jumped up. 'I know,' she said, 'if Fudgie's a doggie he wants to eat on the floor! Right?'

If you ask me Fudge never even thought about that. But he liked the idea a lot. He barked and nodded his head. So my mother fixed his plate and put it under the table. Then she reached down and petted him as though he was a real dog.

My father said, 'Aren't we carrying this a little too far?'

My mother didn't answer.

Fudge ate two bites of his dinner.

My mother was satisfied.

After a week of having him eat under the table

we felt like we really did have a family dog. I thought how great it would be if we could trade in Fudge for a nice cocker spaniel. That would solve all my problems. I'd walk with him and feed him and play with him. He could even sleep on the edge of my bed at night. But of course that was wishful thinking. My brother is here to stay. And there's nothing much I can do about it.

Grandma came over with a million ideas about getting Fudge to eat. She tricked him by making milk shakes in the blender. When Fudge wasn't looking she threw in an egg. Then she told him if he drank it all up there would be a surprise in the bottom of the glass. The first time he believed her. He finished her milk shake. But all he saw was an empty glass. There wasn't any surprise! Fudge got so mad he threw the glass down. It smashed into little pieces. After that Grandma left.

The next day my mother dragged Fudge to Dr Cone's office. He told her to leave him alone. That Fudge would eat when he got hungry.

I reminded my mother that I'd told her the same thing – and for free! But I guess my mother didn't believe either one of us because she took Fudge to see three more doctors. None of them could find a thing wrong with my brother. One doctor even suggested that my mother cook Fudge his favourite foods.

So that night my mother broiled lamb chops just for Fudge. The rest of us ate stew. She served him the two little lamb chops on his plate under the table. Just the smell of them was enough to make my stomach growl. I thought it was mean of my mother to make them for Fudge and not for me.

Fudge looked at his lamb chops for a few minutes. Then he pushed his plate away. 'No!' he said. 'No chops!'

'Fudge . . . you'll starve!' cried my mother cried. 'You *must* eat!'

'No chops! Corn Flakes,' Fudge said. 'Want Corn Flakes!'

My mother ran to get the cereal for Fudge. 'You can eat the chops if you want them, Peter,' she told me.

I reached down and helped myself to the lamb chops. My mother handed Fudge his bowl of cereal. But he didn't eat it. He sat at my feet and looked up at me. He watched me eat his chops.

'*Eat your cereal*' my father said.

'NO! NO EAT CEREAL!' Fudge yelled.

My father was really mad. His face turned bright red. He said, 'Fudge, you will eat that cereal or you will wear it!'

This was turning out to be fun after all, I thought. And the lamb chops were really tasty. I dipped a bone in some ketchup and chewed away.

Fudge messed around with his cereal for a minute. Then he looked at my father and said, 'NO EAT, NO EAT . . . NO EAT!'

My father wiped his mouth with his napkin, pushed back his chair, and got up from the table. He picked up the bowl of cereal in one hand, and Fudge in the other. He carried them both into the bathroom. I went along, nibbling on a bone, to see what was going to happen.

My father stood Fudge in the bath and dumped the whole bowl of cereal right over his head. Fudge screamed. He sure can scream loud.

My father motioned me to go back to the kitchen. He joined us in a minute. We sat down and finished our dinner. Fudge kept on screaming. My mother wanted to go to him but my father told her to stay where she was. He'd had enough of Fudge's monkey business at meal times.

I think my mother really was relieved that my father had taken over. For once my brother got what he deserved. And I was glad!

The next day Fudge sat at the table again. In his little red high chair where he belongs. He ate everything my mother put in front of him. 'No more doggie,' he told us.

And for a long time after that his favourite expression was 'eat it or wear it!'

St Samantha and a Life of Crime

Joan O'Donovan

Brothers and sisters are supposed to love each other. Mum says God said we'd got to, and she nags us when we don't. And I try to love my brother, really I do; it's just that I'm not very good at it. George isn't good at it either, but he doesn't care and I care a lot.

Mum doesn't know I worry about this; but then, I haven't told Mum I want to be a saint. Only my best friend, Emma, who's eight like me, knows that I want to have a saint's career when I leave school. I think it'd be fantastic. I imagine myself doing miracles and blessing people while they curtsey and say, 'Thank you, St Samantha.' In my pretend dreams George doesn't want to curtsey, but I make him and he looks silly, and serve him right. The trouble is, though, they only pick you for a saint if you're really good, and that's hard.

We had our holiday early this year. It was

super going to the seaside while everyone else
was at school, and I promised to bring Emma
back a stick of rock. We stayed at a guest house
called Bella Vista; and George, who's nearly
thirteen, made friends with some boys who'd got
a cricket bat, so he spent most of the time with
them while I played with Mum and Dad. All
went well till the last afternoon, and then Mum
told George he'd got to mind me while she and
Dad went shopping.

We were both furious. We'd have liked to go

shopping, too, but we were skint. I'd got fifty pence, but that was for Emma's rock which I planned to buy next day; and George just can't save. I'm afraid Dad's a bit like George, so it's always Mum who looks after the money and pays our bills.

It was a rotten afternoon. We went on the beach, but there was nothing to do and we weren't talking to each other, and at teatime George made me walk the longest possible way back. I sometimes wish I could get holy and still be allowed not to love George.

We were nearly at Bella Vista when George turned down a side street; and up some steps there was a funny old shop with a bulging front. A sign hung over the door: ANTIQUES.

'What's antikews?' I asked, forgetting I wasn't going to speak first.

'An-*teeks*,' George said, staring hard at something in the window.

I looked, and right at the front, with a ticket on it saying £5.00, I saw a tiny galleon; and, amazingly, *it was inside a bottle*! I gazed at it. I'd never seen anything I wanted so much in all my life.

'How do you get a ship into a bottle like that?' I asked.

'Shove it in flat then pull it up with a string, stupid!'

'Is it hard?'

'I could make dozens,' George said, 'only I wouldn't be bothered.'

So it wasn't the galleon he was looking at.

'George,' I said cautiously, 'if you could have something from here, what would you choose?' and he said without hesitation, 'That stamp, the one on its own in front of the beads.'

'Fancy paying a pound for a used stamp!' I marvelled.

'Don't be so ignorant; that stamp's worth thousands.'

'But it only cost a penny when it was new,' I said reasonably.

'Oh, shut up!' George looked broodingly at the window. 'I just wish I'd got five quid, that's all. I'd know what to do with five quid if I had it.'

'If I'd got five quid I'd buy the ship.'

'I could make you one for a pound,' George suggested, brightening.

'I've only got fifty pence,' I said, feeling for it in my pocket.

'Fancy wanting a dreary old ship anyway!'

'Fancy wanting a used stamp!'

We stared glumly in. An old man came to the door and looked at us.

'If I'd five quid,' George whispered, 'I'd beat that wrinkly down!'

'You mean you'd *hit* him?' I asked fearfully.

'Beat him down means get things cheap – I thought everyone knew that! And I bet he'd let me have everything in his crummy window for five quid.'

'I bet he wouldn't! Why, just the ship costs five pounds.'

'I tell you what,' George said impressively, 'if I beat him down I'll give you that ship for nothing.'

'You wouldn't dare beat him down!'

'I bet you fifty pence I would. *And* you can have the beads as well.'

'All right!' I said excitedly, deciding to take Emma a string of beads instead of rock; and, heart thumping, I gave George my fifty pence.

'Thanks,' George said.

'Well, go on!'

'Go on what?'

'Go on in and beat him down.'

'What, offer the man fifty pence *for all those things*? You're nuts!'

'But you said. . . .'

'I said I *betted* you fifty pence I'd beat him down *if* I had five quid. Well, I haven't got five quid, have I? I've only got fifty pence.'

'You haven't got fifty pence! That fifty pence's mine!' I yelled.

'No it isn't, you've just given it to me,' George said. So I hit him as hard as I could with my wet bikini.

My brother gave a blood-curdling scream.

'You've knocked my eye out!' he shrieked. 'I'm blind!'; and he hid his face in the hand that wasn't holding my money. The old man opened the door and said if we didn't clear off he'd call the police, so we ran away.

By now I was crying. I begged George not to tell Mum that it was I who'd knocked his eye out; and he said he wouldn't if I promised, strike me dead, not to tell her about the fifty pence. So I promised, and George took his hand away and I saw that he'd still got both his eyes.

'Ever been had?' he said, and bought fifty pence worth of sweets.

Next morning I woke up worrying about Emma's rock. I called in for Mum and Dad as usual, but Mum shouted from the shower telling me to go down; as I went, I noticed her money spread out over the table. I'd never seen so much money together before.

And then something awful sort of happened. I found myself hurrying downstairs on wobbly legs with a five-pound note stuffed in my sock.

Dad and George were waiting in the dining room. Dad asked how much pocket money we'd got left.

'None, worst luck!' George grumbled; so Dad smiled and produced two one pound coins. He offered one to me and I went scarlet with shame.

'No, Dad,' I said faintly, 'give it to *Save the Children.*'

'She's nuts!' George said. 'Can I have them both?'

I accepted a pound in the end, to buy Emma's rock. The five pounds was to make George keep his promise to beat the shopkeeper down and give me the ship.

Mum was very late coming for breakfast. She looked pink and upset; and when Dad asked what was wrong she snapped, 'Eat your egg, Arthur!' in that special voice she uses when she's got money worries.

And then I knew. I knew for certain. Mum had missed the five pounds. It had never occurred to me that she'd miss just one note.

'I've had enough,' I said, trying not to tremble.

'Me, too. Can we go?' George asked. 'I want to buy a stamp.'

'Be back by eleven, then!' mother said, glaring at Dad; and for once she forgot to tell George to mind me, and he'd gone before I'd even got down.

I almost reeled to the door. I could feel the money in my sock, and I was afraid Mum might notice the bulge and call me back. And all this misery was for nothing, as I realized now. Involve George? No fear! He'd take one look at the five pound note and tell Mum.

Then I saw a way out. I'd buy the rock *and* the

ship; and if I hid the rock in my suitcase so that nobody saw it, I could pretend I'd beaten the shopkeeper down and got the ship for a pound. Who was to know?

But just before I reached the side street where the shop was, I met George coming back. He showed me his stamp and asked where I was going.

'Mind your own business,' I told him.

'It is my business,' George said, 'I've got to look after you.' So he followed me, and when he wasn't saying how much profit he'd make on the stamp he was offering to help me spend my pound. I daren't go near the antiques shop, so I drifted up and down the front hoping he'd get fed up and go away. But I was the one who got fed up. By half past ten I'd had enough, so I went sulkily up to the kiosk and bought Emma's rock.

George was satisfied then. He'd got his stamp without getting the ship, and he knew I'd no money left.

'Mum didn't say I'd got to mind you *today*,' he said, and scarpered.

As soon as he'd gone I rushed back to the shop. George had seen me buy the rock, of course, so now it was the galleon I'd have to hide: and it dawned on me that a life of crime was more complicated than I'd thought.

Then suddenly I remembered what Mum had

said about a neighbour: 'Tainted money launched her on a life of crime, and now she's a jailbird.'

I stood stock-still on the pavement. A jailbird? Saint Samantha? It was too dreadful to think of! I fished the tainted money out of my sock and pushed it down the drain before it had got time to launch me.

I got back to find Mum and George waiting outside the Bella Vista with our luggage. I could see Mum had been crying.

'Mum thinks Dad's a thief!' George whispered.

'*Dad*? What's he stolen?' I whispered back, horrified.

'Five quid. Only Dad says he didn't; and now he's gone off in a temper and Mum says we'll miss our train.'

My head went light and buzzy, and before I could stop myself I was sick in the bushes. Mum looked at me hard.

'Did *you* take anything from my room, Samantha?' she asked.

'No I didn't! And I feel ill!' I wailed; and then Dad came back with a taxi and we caught the train after all. What's more, Dad managed to persuade Mum that she couldn't have counted the money properly in the first place, so there was peace again – peace, that is, for everyone except me.

I was too miserable to eat, and when we got home I went to bed without any lunch, tea or supper. But in the night, I woke up and couldn't go to sleep again thinking of food. I kept imagining mountains of buttered toast, and baked beans and fish and chips and jam sponge and apple pie; but I knew it'd be hours till breakfast, so when I couldn't bear any more I ate up all of Emma's rock.

I went back to school this morning. I was too embarrassed to speak to Emma, and now Emma won't speak to me so I don't think we'll go on being best friends. I'm still worried about stealing from Mum, too. I know I'll have to confess in the end; but it'd be a lot easier if I hadn't thrown away her five-pound note, which I don't think she'll understand. And that's another thing that's worrying me. I bet they won't pick me for a saint now I've handled tainted money.

George is fed up as well, and serve him right. He took his stamp to a dealer today; but the dealer said he'd been done because it was only worth ten pence, which, George says, means that the wrinkly man made ninety per cent profit.

Ninety per cent! Actually, I'm not quite sure what ninety per cent means; but it does sound an awful lot, so I've decided that if I'm not picked for saint I'm going to keep an antiques shop and get rich.

Acknowledgements

The compilers and publishers wish to thank the following
for permission to use copyright material in this anthology:

J M Dent & Sons for 'Ultra-Violet Catastrophe' by
Margaret Mahy from *Leaf Magic*.

Methuen for 'My Naughty Little Sister and the
Workmen' and 'The Naughtiest Story of All' by
Dorothy Edwards from *My Naughty Little Sister*.

Pixel Publishing (Australia) for 'Jane's Mansion' by
Robin Klein from *Ratbags and Rascals*.

Blackie and Son Limited for 'Having Fun' by
Rene Goscinny from *Nicholas and the Gang at School*.

Collins Publishers for 'Pierre' by Maurice Sendak.

Hodder & Stoughton Limited for 'Mr Miacca' by
Amabel Williams from *The Enchanted World*.

Century Hutchinson for 'Did I Ever Tell You About the
Time When the School Fence was Broken Down?' by
Iris Grender from *The Third Did I Ever Tell You?... Book*.

William Morrow & Company for 'The Christmas List' by
Margaret Rettich from *The Silver Touch and Other Family
Christmas Stories*. Translated from the German by
Elizabeth D. Crawford.

The Bodley Head for 'The Family Dog' by Judy Blume
from *Tales of a Fourth Grade Nothing*.

Joan O'Donovan for 'St Samantha and a Life of Crime'.

Other great reads from **Red Fox**

Further Red Fox titles that you might enjoy reading are listed on the following pages. They are available in bookshops or they can be ordered directly from us.

If you would like to order books, please send this form and the money due to:

ARROW BOOKS, BOOKSERVICE BY POST, PO BOX 29, DOUGLAS, ISLE OF MAN, BRITISH ISLES. Please enclose a cheque or postal order made out to Arrow Books Ltd for the amount due, plus 30p per book for postage and packing, both for orders within the UK and for overseas orders.

NAME _____

ADDRESS _____

_____

Please print clearly.

Whilst every effort is made to keep prices low, it is sometimes necessary to increase cover prices at short notice. If you are ordering books by post, to save delay it is advisable to phone to confirm the correct price. The number to ring is THE SALES DEPARTMENT 071 (if outside London) 973 9700.

Other great reads from Red Fox

THE SNIFF STORIES Ian Whybrow

Things just keep happening to Ben Moore. It's dead hard avoiding disaster when you've got to keep your street cred with your mates *and* cope with a family of oddballs at the same time. There's his appalling 2½ year old sister, his scatty parents who are into healthy eating and animal rights and, worse than all of these, there's Sniff! If only Ben could just get on with his scientific experiments and his attempt at a world beating *Swampbeast* score . . . but there's no chance of that while chaos is just around the corner.

ISBN 0 09 9750406 £2.99

J.B. SUPERSLEUTH Joan Davenport

James Bond is a small thirteen-year-old with spots and spectacles. But with a name like that, how can he help being a supersleuth?

It all started when James and 'Polly' (Paul) Perkins spotted a teacher's stolen car. After that, more and more mysteries needed solving. With the case of the Arabian prince, the Murdered Model, the Bonfire Night Murder and the Lost Umbrella, JB's reputation at Moorside Comprehensive soars.

But some of the cases aren't quite what they seem . . .

ISBN 0 09 9717808 £2.99

Other great reads from **Red Fox**

**Discover the exciting and hilarious books of
Hazel Townson!**

THE MOVING STATUE

One windy day in the middle of his paper round, Jason Riddle
is blown against the town's war memorial statue.

   But the statue moves its foot! Can this be true?

ISBN 0 09 973370 6   £1.99

ONE GREEN BOTTLE

Tim Evans has invented a fantasic new board game called
REDUNDO. But after he leaves it at his local toy shop it
disappears! Could Mr Snyder, the wily toy shop owner have
stolen the game to develop it for himself? Tim and his friend
Doggo decide to take drastic action and with the help of a
mysterious green bottle, plan a Reign of Terror.

ISBN 0 09 956810 1   £2.25

THE SPECKLED PANIC

When Kip buys Venger's Speckled Truthpaste instead of
toothpaste, funny things start happening. But they get out of
control when the headmaster eats some by mistake. What terrible
truths will he tell the parents on speech day?

ISBN 0 09 935490 X   £2.25

THE CHOKING PERIL

In this sequel to *The Speckled Panic,* Herbie, Kip and Arthur
Venger the inventor attempt to reform Grumpton's litterbugs.

ISBN 0 09 950530 4   £2.25

Other great reads from **Red Fox**

School stories from Enid Blyton

THE NAUGHTIEST GIRL IN THE SCHOOL

'Mummy, if you send me away to school, I shall be so naughty there, they'll have to send me back home again,' said Elizabeth. And when her parents won't be budged, Elizabeth sets out to do just that—she stirs up trouble all around her and gets the name of the bold bad schoolgirl. She's sure she's longing to go home—but to her surprise there are some things she hadn't reckoned with. Like making friends . . .

ISBN 0 09 945500 5 £2.99

THE NAUGHTIEST GIRL IS A MONITOR

'Oh dear, I wish I wasn't a monitor! I wish I could go to a monitor for help! I can't even think what I ought to do!'

When Elizabeth Allen is chosen to be a monitor in her third term at Whyteleafe School, she tries to do her best. But somehow things go wrong and soon she is in just as much trouble as she was in her first term, when she was the naughtiest girl in the school!

ISBN 0 09 945490 4 £2.99

Other great reads ⫷ *from* **Red Fox**

AMAZING ORIGAMI FOR CHILDREN
Steve and Megumi Biddle

Origami is an exciting and easy way to make toys, decorations and all kinds of useful things from folded paper.

Use leftover gift paper to make a party hat and a fancy box. Or create a colourful lorry, a pretty rose and a zoo full of origami animals. There are over 50 fun projects in Amazing Origami.

Following Steve and Megumi's step-by-step instructions and clear drawings, you'll amaze your friends and family with your magical paper creations.

ISBN 0 09 9661802 £5.99

MAGICAL STRING   Steve and Megumi Biddle

With only a loop of string you can make all kinds of shapes, puzzles and games. Steve and Megumi Biddle provide all the instructions and diagrams that are needed to create their amazing string magic in another of their inventive and absorbing books.

ISBN 0 09 964470 3   £2.50